This book is dedicated to my ~~~ beautiful, melanin nieces, Malaiya and Mercedes, and the young women who were a part of the Outstanding United Resilient Sisters (O.U.R.S.) mentorship program.

You all encouraged and motivated me to write this book.

I hope this book will encourage young women of color to look in the mirror and say, "I love me!"

— Renita Pagan

Text copyright © 2020 by Renita N. Pagan
Cover art and interior illustrations copyright © 2020 by Ayanna M. Davis

All rights reserved.
Published in the United States by Outstanding United Resilient
Sisters (O.U.R.S.).

ISBN   978-0-578-71543-8

Layout design by Kevin D. Bass Jr.

# Melanin stands for...

Modest

Empowered

Level-headed

Ambitious

Notable

Inspired

Natural

# M is for Modest.

As a young woman of color, you must love your features and know that your body parts are sacred.

E is for Empowered.
Having strength and confidence is key. Be a leader, and build a sisterhood that uplifts, supports, challenges, and motivates each other.

L is for Level-headed.
Brown skin girl, remember that you wear a crown, and when you are level-headed, you have the ability to make great decisions.

# A is for Ambitious.

Hey niece! I want you to be ambitious.
Have a strong desire and determination to
succeed. And flourish into an independent,
powerful, and assertive young woman.

N is for Notable.
Young queen, know that you're worthy of
attention. And you are important enough
to be characterized by distinction and
excellence.

I is for Inspire.
Remember to always be yourself. There is no one else like you, and that's what makes YOU so special! Encourage others to be confident being their unique selves.

# N is for Natural.

Your natural hair, nose, eyes, lips, and complexion is so beautiful. Remain true to yourself and embrace your melanin!

Our hair is full of beautiful curls and coils. Our brown, angelic eyes sparkle. Our full noses and lips are full of love. Our skin drips of melanin and glows in the sun's rays. Melanin is magic!

# My Melanin

Made in the USA
Middletown, DE
02 April 2022

63537480R00015